Walking in the Sky

T0337140

Written by Tom Ottway

Illustrated by Javier Joaquín

Collins

Who and what is in this story?

Listen and say

big leaves

forest

Dad

Mum

Aunt Hazel

Herb

Download the audio at www.collins.co.uk/839701

Maria

hotel

HOTEL

TAXI

taxi

My name is Herb. I like playing computer games at home. It's safe at home – but not always. I don't like flies!

Then Aunt Hazel invited me to go on holiday with her.

That's nice!

Oh!

Hi Herb!
Let's go to a different country for my birthday!
Love, Aunt Hazel
xxx

At the airport, Aunt Hazel had a big smile on her face.

"It's exciting, Herb!" she said. "It's great!"

But I was scared!

"Are the planes safe, Aunt Hazel?" I asked.

"Yes," said Aunt Hazel. "Don't worry!"

My home is in a city. It's cold and grey there. We got off the plane, and it was very different.

The sky was blue and the sun was hot.
I saw tall, green trees. It was beautiful.
Now it was exciting!

We went from the airport in a taxi. The taxi stopped under some trees. A man with fruit picked up a big pineapple and he gave it to me.

"Are you here on holiday?" the man asked.

"Yes," I answered.

"This is for you," he said.

And then he gave Aunt Hazel some watermelon.

"Thank you!" we said.

At the hotel, we found a big swimming pool.

"Let's swim," said Aunt Hazel. She loves swimming!

"Er ... I don't want to," I said.

It's great, Herb!

"Help!" I called. "It's a shark!"

"Don't be silly! It's not a shark!" said
Aunt Hazel.

It was a small boy.

"Oh!" I said. "I thought he was a shark!"

In the morning, after breakfast, I looked out of the bathroom window. It was very, very beautiful.

I saw lots and lots of colours. There was a rainbow and the birds were all the colours of the rainbow. Was it a dream?

Then a woman called Maria took us to the forest.

"You can walk in the forest with me," she said, but I was scared. Snakes live in the forest!

A snake sat on a rock behind a tree with big leaves. I jumped behind Aunt Hazel.

"It's OK!" Maria said. "The snake is more scared than you are!"

It's beautiful!

The holiday was fantastic and exciting.
I loved it! But then Maria said, "Let's go
up the Stairs to the Sky!"

At the top of the Stairs to the Sky, I closed my eyes. I was scared!

"I can't do it!" I said.

"It's OK," said Aunt Hazel. "Open your eyes. You're safe with us."

I put my left foot down, then my right foot. I started walking.

"Yes! Well done, Herb!" said Aunt Hazel. "You're walking in the sky!"

I did it!

We're at home now. It's cold and wet and it's not very exciting, but I like the garden.

Picture dictionary

Listen and repeat

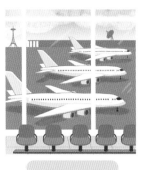

airport

computer game

fly

hotel

rainbow

scared

taxi

1 Look and order the story

2 Listen and say

Collins

Published by Collins
An imprint of HarperCollins*Publishers*
Westerhill Road
Bishopbriggs
Glasgow
G64 2QT

HarperCollins*Publishers*
1st Floor, Watermarque Building
Ringsend Road
Dublin 4
Ireland

William Collins' dream of knowledge for all began with the publication of his first book in 1819.

A self-educated mill worker, he not only enriched millions of lives, but also founded a flourishing publishing house. Today, staying true to this spirit, Collins books are packed with inspiration, innovation and practical expertise. They place you at the centre of a world of possibility and give you exactly what you need to explore it.

© HarperCollins*Publishers* Limited 2020

10 9 8 7 6 5 4 3 2

ISBN 978-0-00-839701-2

www.collins.co.uk/elt

British Library Cataloguing in Publication Data

A catalogue record for this publication is available from the British Library.

Author: Tom Ottway
Illustrator: Javier Joaquín (Beehive)
Series editor: Rebecca Adlard
Commissioning editor: Fiona Undrill
Publishing manager: Lisa Todd
Product managers: Jennifer Hall and Caroline Green
In-house editor: Alma Puts Keren
Project manager: Emily Hooton
Editor: Matthew Hancock
Proofreaders: Natalie Murray and Michael Lamb
Cover designer: Kevin Robbins
Typesetter: 2Hoots Publishing Services Ltd
Audio produced by id audio, London
Reading guide author: Emma Wilkinson
Production controller: Rachel Weaver
Printed and bound by: GPS Group, Slovenia

Download the audio for this book and a reading guide for parents and teachers at www.collins.co.uk/839701